KRAKEN

COLORING BOOK FOR KIDS

Lucy Z. Brown

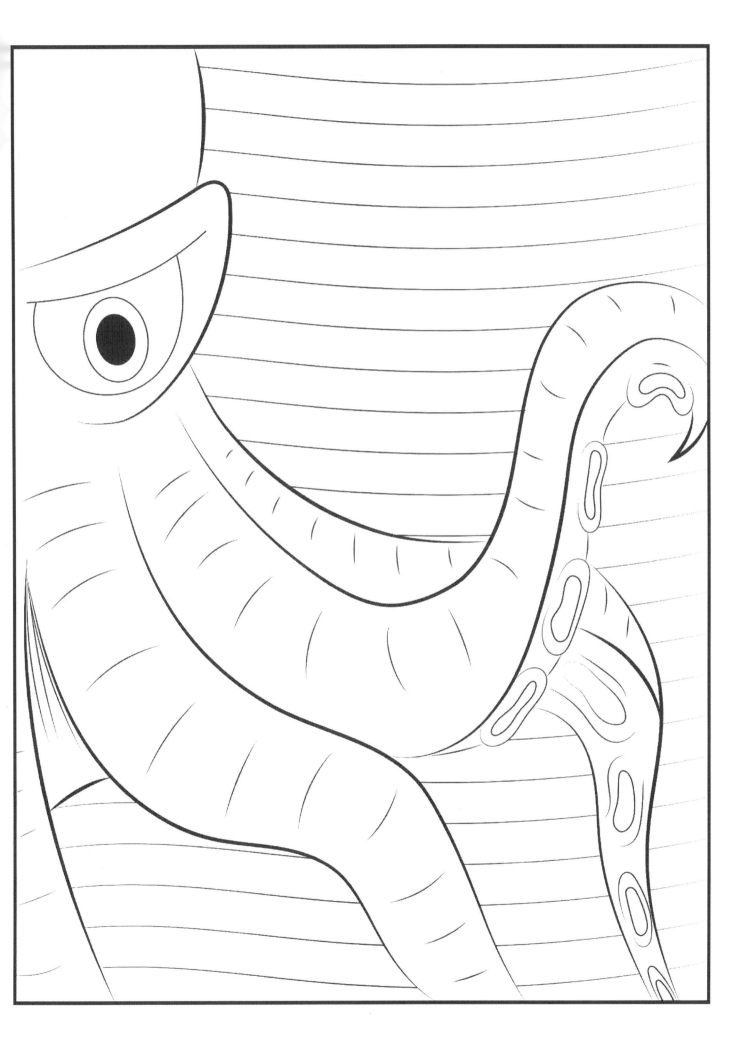

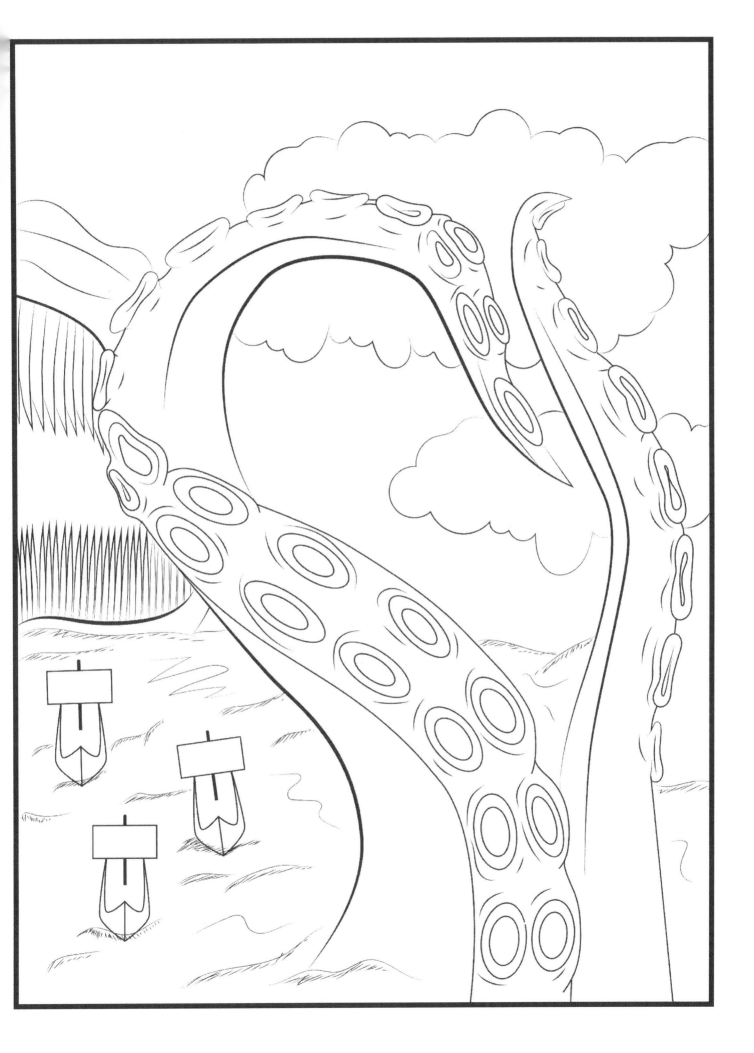

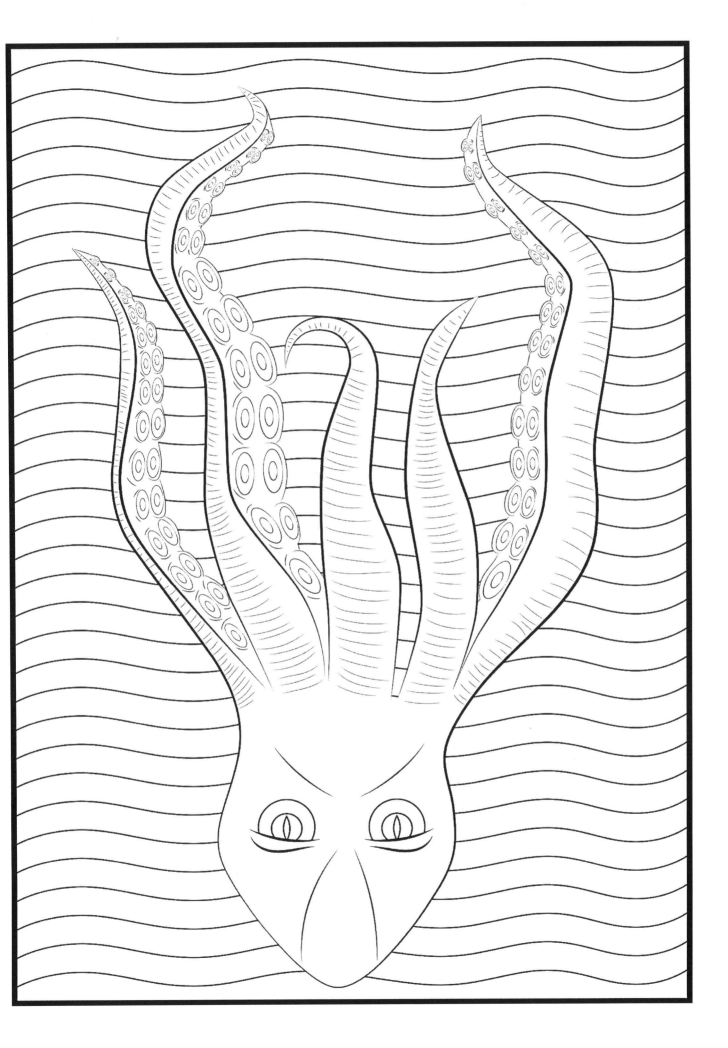

VERY DIFFICULT, COLORING WITH THE HELP OF YOUR PARENTS

VERY DIFFICULT, COLORING WITH THE HELP OF YOUR PARENTS

VERY DIFFICULT, COLORING WITH THE HELP OF YOUR PARENTS

SECOND CHANCE TO COLOR DIFFERENTLY

SECOND CHANCE TO COLOR DIFFERENTLY

SECOND CHANCE TO COLOR DIFFERENTLY

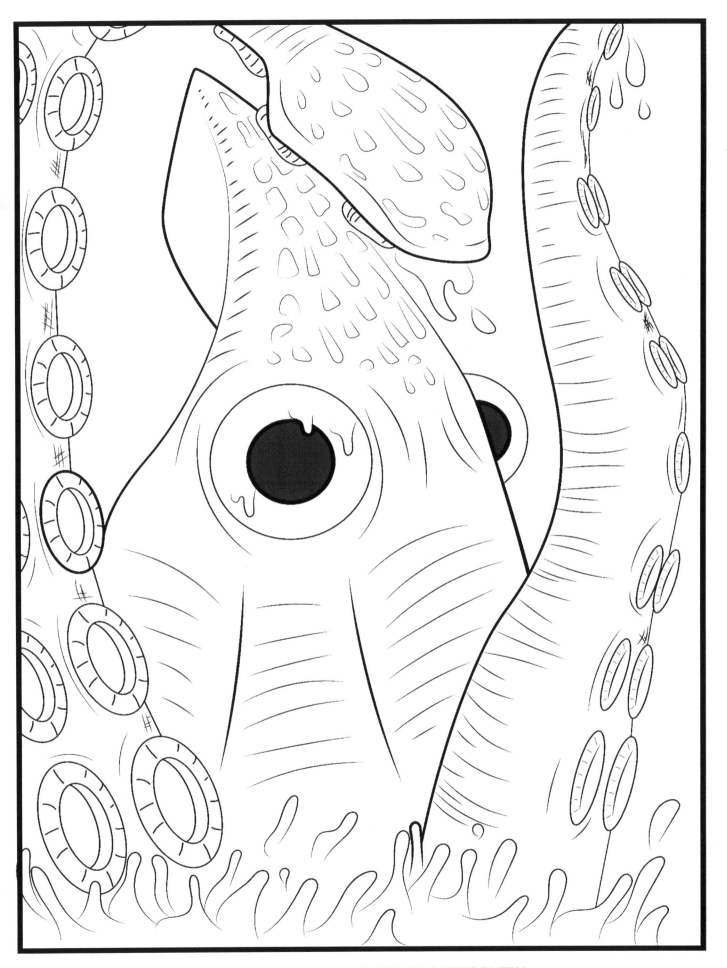

SECOND CHANCE TO COLOR DIFFERENTLY

VERY DIFFICULT, COLORING WITH THE HELP OF YOUR PARENTS

Thank you so much for purchasing this book. If you enjoyed it, then please leave an Amazon review. Reviews are the lifeblood of our publishing endeavors- leaving a positive review would mean the world to us.

Cheers!

-Lucy Z. Brown

Made in the USA
Columbia, SC
08 October 2024